For Kitty and Kate
D. M.

For Deirdre and Lucy
S. H.

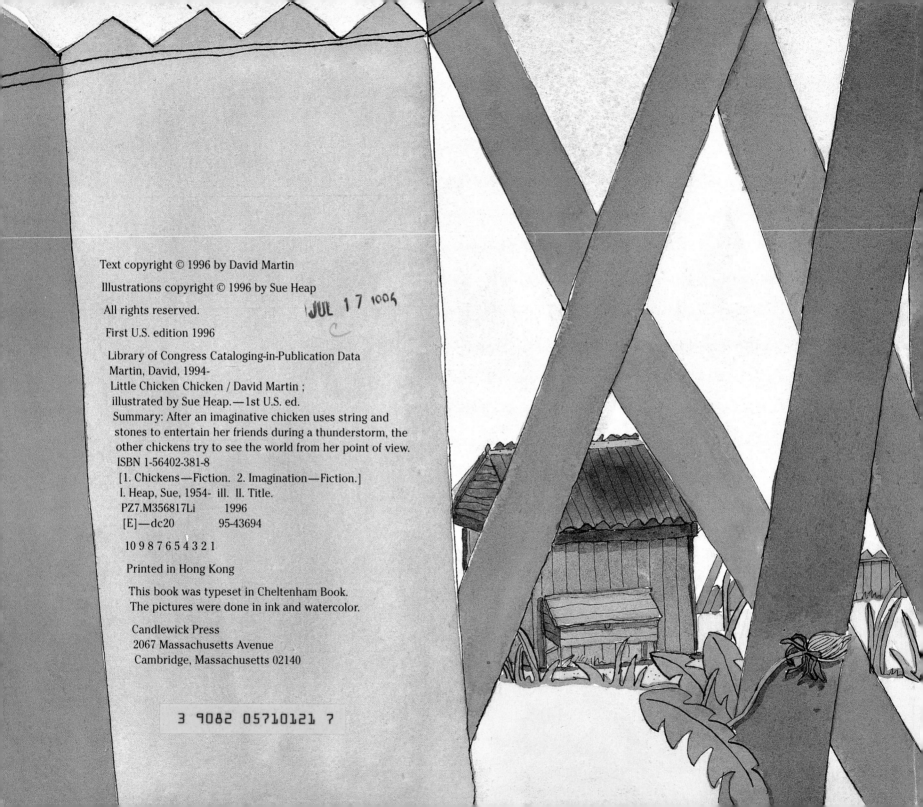

JUL 17 1006

First U.S. edition 1996

Library of Congress Cataloging-in-Publication Data
Martin, David, 1994-
Little Chicken Chicken / David Martin ;
illustrated by Sue Heap.—1st U.S. ed.
Summary: After an imaginative chicken uses string and
stones to entertain her friends during a thunderstorm, the
other chickens try to see the world from her point of view.
ISBN 1-56402-381-8
[1. Chickens—Fiction. 2. Imagination—Fiction.]
I. Heap, Sue, 1954- ill. II. Title.
PZ7.M356817Li   1996
[E]—dc20   95-43694

10 9 8 7 6 5 4 3 2 1

Printed in Hong Kong

This book was typeset in Cheltenham Book.
The pictures were done in ink and watercolor.

Candlewick Press
2067 Massachusetts Avenue
Cambridge, Massachusetts 02140

LITTLE CHICKEN CHICKEN

David Martin

illustrated by Sue Heap

CANDLEWICK PRESS
CAMBRIDGE, MASSACHUSETTS

Little Chicken Chicken and Baby Chick were scratching in the garden with the other chickens.

"Look," said Little Chicken Chicken, "I found a string. I'm going to make a tightrope out of it."

"That's nice, dear," said her mother.

The other chickens looked up and laughed at Little Chicken Chicken.

"Some tightrope!" they said.

Little Chicken Chicken put her string in a box

inside the chicken coop and started doing backflips.

The next day she found
two round black stones.

"Look at these stones,"
she said. "They fell out
of a thundercloud.
See, that's why
they're so dark."

"Oh, *really*," said the rooster. And he and the big chickens all laughed.

Then the little chickens
began to tease her.

One of them had a bent nail.
"Here's another thundercloud,
Silly Chicken Chicken."

"And here's some wind,"
they said. And they blew
dandelion fluff at her.

That afternoon,
Little Chicken Chicken
found a sparkling glass bead.
She put it away with her
other toys and didn't tell
anyone about it.

Soon the wind picked up and ruffled the chickens' feathers. "Feels like it's going to rain," said Little Chicken Chicken's mother.

Lightning flashed and thunder shook the ground.

It began to rain hard.

The chickens ran into the coop and huddled together. Suddenly the wind blew away a piece of the roof.

"Ahhh!" screamed the little chickens, and they began to cry.

"Help!" screamed the big chickens, and they began to shake.

"Oh," said Little Chicken Chicken, "my toys are getting soaked!" She flew down to save them and then began to play.

She strung up her string, hopped onto it, and balanced on one foot.

"Look," someone whispered. "Look at Little Chicken Chicken."

And as lightning lit up the coop, she did a backflip off the string . . .

and a cartwheel across the floor!

The rooster applauded.
"Ladies and gentlemen," he said,
"it's Little Chicken Chicken's
Thunderstorm Circus."
"Do more. Do more,"
everyone said. "Please."

So Little Chicken Chicken jumped back up on the string. She held up her two black stones and said, "My friends, these stones are from the heart of a thundercloud."

And then, with a wave of her wing, she made the sparkling glass bead appear. "And this is a piece of lightning I grabbed as it flashed across the sky."

"These things are so magical they will fly in the air before your very eyes."

And she tossed them up and began to juggle.

Everyone cheered.

Soon all the chickens were doing backflips and trying to juggle and falling off the string.

"Was that true? Did that bead really come from lightning?" Baby Chick asked her mother.

"I don't know. Ask Little Chicken Chicken."

But just then the rain stopped
and everyone went outside.

"Look, I found a thunder-
stone," said one little chicken.

"Me too," said another. "And I
found a piece of lightning."

But Little Chicken Chicken didn't hear them.

She was too busy chasing grasshoppers.

"Watch out!" she shouted.

"Leaping dino-monstersaurs!"

"Wait for us!"

the other chickens said.

And off they went,

jumping and shouting

and flapping across

the garden.